A WEE BIT OF TROUBLE

A Wee Bit of Trouble

Mike Church

illustrations by Louise Richards

Pont

For Herb and Mary, Liz, Julian, Carla,
Fay and Jake

'Imagination is more important than knowledge'

Albert Einstein

First published in 2013 by Pont Books, an imprint of
Gomer Press, Llandysul, Ceredigion, SA44 4JL
www.gomer.co.uk

ISBN 978 1 84851 671 7

A CIP record for this title is available from the British Library.

This book is published with the financial support of the
Welsh Books Council.

Printed and bound in Wales at Gomer Press,
Llandysul, Ceredigion

CONTENTS

A WEE BIT OF TROUBLE

I'm sure you all had a teacher like Mrs Grimwood
who should not have taught
but *fought* for her country.
Picture now school assembly:
varnished bottoms on varnished floors
and teachers guarding all the doors
as Mrs Grimwood bashed out
All Things Bright and Beautiful,
whilst I sat there, bursting to go
but trying to slow
my bladder's urge,
then a surge,
I couldn't wait.
Too late.
I did a wee into my grey shorts and beyond,
an unstoppable pond
and, as the puddle grew,
and children knew,
they withdrew.

I became a little island of guilt
as they built
a moat around me
until Mrs G could see,
and, amidst clouds of steam and tears,
all my worst fears
came true.
'You!' she cried,

the worst of teachers
for all creatures
great and small.
I had to stand in front of the whole school,
a weak-bladdered fool.
'And let this be a lesson to you all!
Do not come into the hall
needing the toilet
or you'll spoil it
for everyone else.'

This assembly is a lesson for you
and a lesson for me.
If you ever need a wee,
make sure Mrs G
can't see.
Because wherever you go
and whatever you do,
Mrs Grimwood will be watching you.
Always!

THE BEST DAYS OF YOUR LIFE

My gran always says
'Enjoy your childhood.
These are the best days of your life.'
But she's been a wife
and a mother
and now she's a gran
so how can
I enjoy my childhood
with nothing to reflect on?
My years haven't come and gone.
I mean, I'm sorry, Gran,
I'll do what I can
and I'm sure one day
I'll look back and say
it was great
(when it's probably too late)
but at this minute
when I'm right here in it
I'm too busy playing
to be sat here saying
'These are the best days of my life.'

SCAREDY-CAT

I'm not really scared of anything.

I mean, obviously, when Miss said
a lady was coming from the reptile centre
I expected a tortoise or maybe a lizard –
I didn't know she'd have a python,
and of course I didn't want to touch it.
I mean, I might have got snake flu
or the slithering lurgy.
And then when she pulled out a tarantula
I didn't want it crawling on me.
I mean, it's not really a reptile, is it?
So I didn't see the point.

I'm not really scared of anything.

I mean, obviously, Josh Wicks in Year Six
is a big boy but I'm not really scared of him –
just because he plays rugby for the Ospreys
under-sixteens
when he's only eleven,
and he's already started shaving.
I would tell him to keep the noise down if he
was noisy
but I wouldn't say he's noisy exactly, just a bit chatty.

I mean, I'm not really scared of anything.

And, yes, sometimes my mum leaves the landing
light on
but that's not because I'm scared of the dark,
it's in case there's an emergency in the night
and, yes, I do get someone to check behind the door
and under the bed and in the wardrobe
before I go to sleep.
But that's just plain common sense, isn't it?

I'm not really scared of anything.

My friend Dewi Miles says
everyone's scared of something,
and it's braver to admit you're scared.

But I'm scared to admit
I'm scared of anything,
in case they call me a scaredy-cat.
Because I'm not really scared of anything
. . . not really.

THE SUN HAS GOT HIS HAT ON

We had a science lesson today
and we heard Miss say
in a throwaway remark (our bin is full of them)
that the earth would one day be dark
when the sun burns itself out,
expands, expires and dies.
I hope this is lies
because, if the sun goes, then so will we,
and then I can't see
the point of finishing my project on the planets.

GOSSIP COLUMN

I'm not one to gossip
but when Dewi Miles
kissed Glenys Giles
she'd already kissed Lewis Pugh
too
on the same day
in exactly the same way.
So when I heard Dewi say
'Glenys Giles is all mine',
I wanted to tell him of the crime –
of her kissing two boys in one break –
and somehow shake
him of talk of them being together
forever
because Glenys Giles treats us boys
like toys.
And I thought I might invite
Dewi to my house for tea,
but I could see
he wasn't interested in playing,
he was going to Glenys's instead.
I felt my face go red
(I didn't know what to do)
so I told Dewi about Lewis Pugh,
which caused a fight
about who was right
for Glenys Giles, all smiles.

Then Dewi stormed off with me
to my house for tea,
and we played football in the park
till it was almost dark,
and the very next day
during afternoon play
I heard Glenys say
she was in love with *me*!
So when no one could see
I gave her a kiss
and told nobody about this . . .
'cos I'm not one for gossip.

AGE APPROPRIATE

This poem is for children, like me,
who are exactly ten (and three-quarters),
if you are not ten (and three-quarters)
please stop reading this poem now,
but if you are ten (and three-quarters)
you know exactly what I'm talking about,
so I don't need to say another word.

BOYS DON'T READ

Boys don't read,
they dream of hat tricks and Hadron Colliders
of chemicals and computer games
and scoring winning tries for Wales.
Hibernating in quilts,
they inhabit a post-nuclear world
of underwater cityscapes
where they destroy endless mutant zombies
and save the universe
from psychopathic grenade-launching grannies
in high definition.
Gangly gangsters with gadgets,
boys don't read,
they are buried in hoodies
on roller skates and roller blades
doing parkour and press-ups,
testing their testosterone,
terminating bystanders and buying
burger baps and beige daps.
Boys don't read,
they reinvent wheels
with chrome-trimmed exhausts,
blowing drum and bass through the vibrating
windows
of the once-and-future young.
They speed
through their adolescence and arrive
without a book in sight.

Boys don't read,
but if they did
the world would be a different place –
less black and white,
more grey
and softer round the edges.

MAKING CONVERSATION

'Ere, you seen that bald bloke in the library?'

'No. What about him?'

'Well he's bald.'

'So what?'

'Well I was only saying.'

'Yeah but why say it?'

'Well I was just making conversation.'

'But that's not conversation, that's just stating the
   obvious.'

'No it's not . . . 'cos you haven't seen him, have you?'

'No I haven't, but that still doesn't make it a
   conversation starter.'

'Yes it does.'

'No it doesn't.'

'But we're having a conversation now, aren't we?'

'No, we're having an argument now!'

'No we're not.'

'Yes we are!'

'Are we? . . . Well, what's it about then?'

'Some bald bloke in the library!'

'But I thought you hadn't seen him?'

'I haven't!'

'So why are we arguing about it then?'

'That's it! Don't ever speak to me again.'

'Why not?'

''Cos you do my head in, that's why.'

'Well at least you're not bald.'

ANY QUESTIONS?

Miss, you know when you asked us
to all put our hands up,
and then the light came on?
And you said
'There you are, children, always remember
many hands make light work',
that's not really how light works, is it, Miss?
How does light work, Miss?
And you know when you said
about the World Wide Web and you said
'Just imagine the size of the World Wide Spider',
there isn't really a spider that big, is there, Miss?
And when I pulled that face
at Megan Davies and you said
if I wasn't careful my face might stay like it,
that's not true, is it, Miss?
Because I forgot what you said
and made that face three times during break
and I don't look any different, do I, Miss?
And when your husband came to the Christmas
concert
and he's completely bald, Miss, isn't he?
And you said it's because the hair fairies came
and stole it all and left 30p under his pillow
but there aren't really such things as hair fairies,
are there?
And they'd leave more than 30p, wouldn't they, Miss?

And you know you said
you're too busy to talk to me?
Well you're not really, are you, Miss,
because you've been sat there
with your eyes closed doing nothing, Miss,
though you've been counting to ten again
and again.
Why is that, Miss?
You don't mind me asking all these questions,
do you, Miss?
Miss . . . ?

SWAPS AND STEALS

When Rhian Moore stole my rubber,
I wanted to club her,
but Miss says hitting is bad
(especially when you're mad)
so I counted to ten,
thought about it again,
and asked for it back
but she'd given it to Jack.
I counted to ten once more
but he'd thrown it on the floor,
where Lowri Price sneaked it away
and, during afternoon play,
swapped it with Josh Wicks
(the big boy in Year Six).
Nightmare! Unfair!
When I plucked up courage to ask Josh
all he said was 'Oh my gosh,
I swapped my best swapping card for this!'
but luckily, just then, Miss
(who'd overhead it all)
said we had to undo all swaps.
That's why teachers are tops –
they don't miss a trick,
though I did nick Rhian Moore's pen –
now *she'll* have to count to ten!

PLEASE MISS

Please, Miss,
I know you told us to bring in our reading books
but I haven't got mine, Miss,
'cos when I got home
my older brother rolled it up to use as a pea-shooter
and he shot the lady next door
and she complained to the police
and they wanted it as evidence
but my mum said 'No!' 'cos I needed it for school
and she grabbed it with the policeman
and they wrestled and tore it in half, Miss.
My sister said she'd glue it together, Miss,
but she managed to superglue half of it
to a plate of pasta she was eating
then decided the other half was no good any more
so she lined her hamster's cage with it, Miss,
and he messed on it, Miss . . . and that ruined page 7,
then he tore up the rest for a den in his cage.
My mum chucked the other half, with the plate,
in the bin
but during the night, Miss, you'll never guess,
we got broken into by thieves
and they stole the hamster, his cage, and our bin,
Miss,
(I don't know why).
Anyway we called the police, Miss,
but they didn't want to come

'cos the policeman had been injured wrestling with
my mum
and anyway he said we're a family that always
tells lies.
But we don't, Miss, honest we don't.
So can I have a new book please, Miss?
'Cos I've told the truth now, haven't I, Miss!

ROLLERCOASTER THERAPY

When I'm down,
with a full-length frown,
I love to ride the rollercoaster.
I'm not a rollercoaster boaster
who raises his arms at every drop,
and never wants it to stop,
I just love the way I'm thrown around
with a rattling, screaming sound
in which I'm totally lost,
pitched about and tossed.
Nothing else matters
as every car clatters
and jumps and jolts
then finally halts.
Then I'm no longer sad,
just alive – and glad!

LOST

A penguin
gets lost,
ends up in Swansea.
Some children
leave him out of games.
Some children
call him names
and say
he smells of fish.
But some children
take him
under their wing
and call him
'the Emperor'
which, of course,
he is.

ACTION POEM

I want to write an action poem
where there's an earthquake in the second line
and a four-car pile-up in line three.

I want to write an action poem
where mushroom clouds invade kitchens,
snogged frogs turn into caterpillars
and vice versa,
where the evolving world spins and dries
as the moon hurdles tidal waves
and God walks into town with a six-pack
and a bazooka.

I want to write an action poem
with speed-boat chases
and grenade-launching granddads
cascading from an exploding chest of drawers.

I want to write an action poem
where teachers pull teeth
and children never listen.
It's got hurricanes and twisting tornadoes,
dragons and deadly viruses.

I want to write an action poem
but Sir says it has to be about autumn.

WHEN THE WIND BLOWS

Mrs Bevan broke wind today
but we were all too polite to say
'pardon you',
though Lewis Pugh
(who's new)
opened a window
to let her know
we'd heard.
It's occurred
before
and at sixty-four
Mrs Bevan is nearly retired.
She shouldn't be fired,
she hasn't sinned,
just broken wind
as she pinned
a poem to the wall.
Happens to us all.

'TWAS ON THE CUSP OF BEDTIME

Miss says I'm easily led
but when it's time for bed
I'm not going anywhere.
I sit on the bottom stair,
eating a chocolate finger,
but Mum won't let me linger,
says it's taking far too long.
I say she's wrong –
a biscuit needs love and care,
it needs to be eaten slow
or else I'll go
to bed with indigestion.
So the suggestion
that I'm stalling for time
is a crime
'cos eating chocolate fingers is an art.
I can't start
and finish too quick
or I'll be sick.
Then Mum takes me by the arm and says
'I've seen you eat a packet of biscuits
without stopping to chew,
that's quite enough from you!'
And with that I'm led, easily,
straight up to bed.

ON THE M4

The teachings of Mohammed and Jesus,
the passion of Martin Luther King,
the simple truth of Gandhi,
all that has gone before
means nothing on the M4.
My mum and dad do not drive gently by day or night,
they rage, rage at every car in sight.
It is the dying of the light.
The teachings of Mohammed and Jesus,
the passion of Martin Luther King,
the simple truth of Gandhi,
all that has gone before
means nothing on the M4.

READING ALOUD

Please don't make me read aloud
in front of all these people.
I'd rather walk on hot coals or across a frozen lake
or wrestle a lion and give it a shake.
I'd rather juggle eggs that aren't hard-boiled
or poke my head where a python's coiled
but please don't make me read aloud
in front of all these people.

I'll wash your car and behave like a saint,
give you my last Rolo without complaint,
you can have the coat right off my back
or I'll climb the beanstalk instead of Jack,
but please don't make me read aloud
in front of all these people.

You can have my Xbox or PlayStation 3,
you can come to my house and eat my tea,
I'll mow your lawn or hold your coat,
if you want it, you can have my vote,
I'll make you meals I can't even cook
or say 'it was me' and get you off the hook,
I'll pop to the shop and buy you bread,
or plump the pillows on your bed,
I'll carry your case to Timbuktu
or do just anything for you,
but please, please don't make me read aloud
in front of all these people.

WORN OUT

My mum never knows what to wear.
She goes up and down each stair,
saying, 'Do I look good in this,
or do I look good in that?'
She's just convinced herself she's fat,
so I told her about the Emperor's New Clothes
and she said, 'Oh no, I wouldn't look good in those!'

A BIT FISHY

My mum insists I take Omega Three
but, as I'm blinking
back fishy burps,
and taking slurps
of saltwater,
I can't see
what this does for me.
She says it increases my intelligence,
makes me focussed and clear-thinking.
I don't want these pills.
Now I'm growing gills,
I'm dreaming of whales
and developing scales!
Though improved as a swimmer
I can't eat a fish dinner!
My mouth opens and closes
if you mention bottlenoses.
If God wanted cod
I'd be floundering in the sea
as Omega Three!
So no more of these pills
improving my head –
just give me a few Maltesers instead.

BRIEF THOUGHTS
ON BEING ASSERTIVE
(or do the meek really inherit the earth?)

Timid Tina and Timid Tom
never say boo to a goose,
they are the last two
in every queue,
and every day
the dinner ladies say
to Timid Tina and Timid Tom:
'Sorry, loves, it's all gone.'

POETRY WRITING

I love stomping through puddles
and blowing bubbles in a glass of milk,
I love lying in bed and dreaming of faraway places
with bazaars and camels and runaway baps,
I love watching Olympic skiers crash and crumple
into advertising hoardings.
I love running my finger through the icing on a cake
and writing my name on a steamed-up window,
I love having the whole settee to myself
or finishing off the last chocolate in the box.
I love wobbling a jelly on a plate
or the smell of a roasting Sunday dinner,
I love knocking doors and running away
or reading under the bedclothes by torchlight.
But one thing I absolutely hate
is someone giving me
a piece of paper and saying,
'Write a poem right there, right now.'

I can't stand that.

JEALOUS? ME?

I'm not jealous of Bleddyn Roberts.
Jealousy is a bad thing
that eats away at you,
gnaws at your very soul.

I'm not jealous of Bleddyn Roberts.
He's just a boy who has it all –
expensive flash trainers
Billabong, Bench and Quiksilver,
the latest iPhone, PlayStation
PSP, Wii and Xbox.

You name it,
he's got it.
You name it,
he's seen it.
You name it,
he's been there.

I'm not jealous of Bleddyn Roberts.
All the girls in school adore him,
all the boys want to be his friend,
all the teachers praise him.
He's captain of the school rugby team
and understands Albert Einstein.

I'm not jealous of Bleddyn Roberts.
I just sincerely believe he should move schools –
a boy with that much talent really needs
to share himself around
less fortunate areas of the town.
It pains me to think
some people have never met him.

I'm not jealous of Bleddyn Roberts.
I just sincerely believe
he should move schools
. . . today!

WASP ATTACK

It came in during maths
and hung around by the paint pots,
but having sampled the purple and blue
it flew in further
and landed on our class globe.
It walked around India for a bit
and had just entered Afghanistan
when chaos erupted.
Myfanwy Hawkins screamed,
which set off three copycat howlers,
Dewi Miles flapped a ruler at it
and Ifor Richards ran to the stock cupboard to hide.
Miss called for calm,
saying things like 'It's only a wasp',
but, for once, nobody listened.
It was Megan Davies who saved the day.
It landed on her arm
and she casually walked to the window,
opened it and let it out.
There was a gasp and a shout.
Megan Davies changed overnight
from being the quiet, shy girl in the corner
to a cross between
Emmeline Pankhurst and Lara Croft.
I was so impressed. At playtime
I asked her to be my girlfriend . . .
but she told me to buzz off!

REPEATING THINGS

Repeating things
repeating things

Is good for you
is good for you

It does no harm
it does no harm

In fact it's fun
in fact it's fun

But don't repeat this
but don't repeat this

No, I mean stop repeating now
no, I mean stop repeating now

Look, it's not funny anymore
look, it's not funny anymore

You still there?
you still there?

It's the end of the page
it's the end of the page.

SECOND CHANCE

Billy Potts mitched off on a Tuesday
when his father was released from prison.
Billy didn't return until Thursday
and he looked thirty-five years old.
Someone said it was Billy's dad
in disguise
as apparently he didn't make the most
of his time in education.
Luckily ours is a school
that believes in making mistakes
and giving second chances.

SCHOOL FÊTE
WITH THE WRITING SQUAD

The music pounds,
a policeman plods,
people pray for sun,
eat burgers and baps
on backless bales . . .

And the writing group writes on.

Cones and cornets,
Gurkhas and greyhounds,
pushchairs and prams,
tugs of war (and love),
rapping and rugby . . .

And the writing group writes on.

Dragons in the sports arena,
docile donkeys,
a moustachioed cream-doughnut girl,
a man in a Motorhead T-shirt,
tattooed and tribal,
a blueberry-smoothie-blending bike,
the Carnival Queen surveying her empire
of balloons and bouncy castles
and a red-belted burger-armed Taekwondo-boy
raising his arm in hunger . . .

And the writing group writes on

about anoraks and pushchairs,
grinning, face-painted tigers,
hot dogs on leads,
trapeze artists and sing-a-long fitness fanatics
up to their knees
in the Ponty puddle.
And in those muddied waters
a reflection of spirit,
community spirit,
where people look out
for one another's shared history.

The school fête will have come and gone
but the writing group writes on.

THE LIBRARY

Go on, take a risk,
cross the threshold,
take a first step,
go on, enter a library.
The Great War, the Great Depression,
the Greatest Goal,
a warehouse, a safe house, a house of horrors
where fact becomes fiction
and vice versa.
From Frankenstein to Hitler
every life recorded,
every life counts.
Go on, enter a library,
research a raisin or a reason we're alive,
explore space the final frontier,
technology and time,
poets and storytellers,
wrestling and wildlife,
plumbers and dinosaurs,
the World Wide Web.
Find out,
find out about this or that, him or her,
find yourself,
fall in love,
the Big Bang, the next big thing,
the main street, the side street.

Find out,
go on, enter a library,
streamlined shelves of shared spaces,
voluptuously veiled volumes,
fascists and crime,
religion and rhyme.
Go on, enter a library,
communal knowledge,
a free college,
of googles, boogles and zoogles.

The world is an oyster,
so come with me,
come on, take a risk,
enter a library.

A BLOKE WITH A JOKE

I'm one of those blokes
who love bad jokes:
What's the difference between a fireman and
a soldier?
You can't dip a fireman in your egg,
and, what do you call a camel with three humps?
Humphrey!
Why did the burglar cut the legs off his bed?
Because he wanted to lie low for a while.
What do you call a woodpecker without a beak?
A head-banger.
What's orange and sounds like a parrot?
A carrot.
Where would you find a dog with no legs?
Exactly where you left it.
Two lions walking through Tesco on a Saturday,
one says to the other,
'Quiet in here for a Saturday, isn't it?'
Two parrots sitting on a perch,
one says to the other,
'Can you smell fish?'
Why do witches ride broomsticks?
Because vacuum cleaners are far too heavy.
Why did the girl take the pencil to bed?
Was she really going to draw the curtains?
And what is bread anyway but just raw toast?

What do you call a three-legged donkey?
A wonky!
Jokes galore,
I've plenty more
and if you winced
then you're convinced
I'm one of those blokes
who love bad jokes.
But when I've finished telling them
I can sit where I like on the bus!

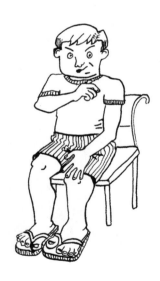

WANT 'N' GREED

I want that,
I want that!

Give it to me,
Give it to me!

Give it,
Give it!

Thank you.

I don't want it now.

COLIN

My friend Colin
says he's played rugby for Wales
but I know he's not actually Welsh
although he claims he's a Welsh-Afghan cross
but he's not Afghan,
that's a dog they had
which the RSPCA took from them.
Colin says his dad's an RSPCA inspector
but he's on the 'never should own a pet' list.
And as for lists –
Colin says he's got:
James Bond's autograph,
a film of a ghost in his attic,
a ripped Lotto ticket that could have won
£100 million,
a great-great-uncle who won five Victoria crosses
at Rorke's Drift,
two talking tortoises,
a tooth from a great white shark
that attacked him on Bondi Beach
and he's also a black belt in karate
although he's apparently so good
he can't do it in case he kills someone.
If my friend Colin
told me he was captain
of the Welsh exaggeration team
I'd actually believe him . . .
but he's never said that.

ANOTHER STRANGE MEETING

I met God quite by chance
at Taff's Well station
late one night, and I'd missed
the last train to Merthyr.
Questions swam round my mind –
why would he be going to Merthyr Tydfil?
Could he take me there now on a miracle?
Would he talk to me?

I knew opportunities like this
don't come by in an average lifetime
but also thought he may be sick of people
always badgering him because of his celebrity.
Are we only allowed to talk to God through prayer?
One-way traffic?

I sauntered over casually,
the weight of the world on my shoulders.
I wanted to ask him why he was a man
and not a woman.
Does he believe in equal opportunities?

I wanted to ask him, obviously,
if he invented everything
then who created him?
I wanted to ask him why three-quarters of the
world starves?
What are the chances of toast landing butter-side up?

Why do leopards have spots
and tigers stripes?
Why does garlic smell the way it does?
Will I go to heaven?
What will Saturday's lottery numbers be?

I wanted to ask so much,
fit to burst,
I sauntered over casually,
the weight of the world on my shoulders,
but the moment I got to him
a taxi pulled up, he jumped in
and disappeared, just like that,
didn't offer me a lift.

There is a lesson for me somewhere,
but for the life of me
I don't know what it is.

READING RECIPE FOR BOYS

Chill with three average Welsh boys,
peel them away from computer games,
scatter and sprinkle books
drizzled in action and adventure,
add two large trolls and a touch of goblin,
remove the head of a tribal chief
and ensure the opening pages
are piping hot and meaty
with a story that sizzles,
soaked in a coating of good and evil.
Cover with mystery and myth
then simmer for ten more pages
until the three average Welsh boys are hooked.
Then serve them to society,
as fluent, well-adjusted readers.

PICKED ON

People pick on you if you're too tall
or just that little bit too small.
They don't like freckles
or the wrong trainers.
They don't like it if you lose.
They don't like it if you win.
They don't like ginger.
They don't like smart.
They don't like too popular
or too pretty for a start.
They don't like ugly,
they don't like good,
they don't like Goths
or if you wear a hood.
They pick on people in glasses
or if you've got big ears.
They pick on you with spiders
if that's one of your fears.
They pick on you if you've got nine toes
(or eleven).
They pick on you
if you say you don't believe in heaven,
or if you do.
They pick on you
if you don't like Man United
or if your granddad's old
and partially sighted.

They pick on you
if you pull funny faces
or cry in films
in all the wrong places.
They pick on you
if you live in one part of town
or another.
They pick on you for having
a little sister or brother.
They pick on you
if you're white or brown or blue.
There's always a reason
to pick on you.
So I've invented
this completely new game
where we all treat everyone
exactly the same.
It's a strange idea,
revolutionary I know,
but go on, smile,
and give it a go.

PLEASE DON'T CHOOSE ME

Have you ever put your hand up,
desperate to be chosen,
and when you are your mind is frozen?
It completely empties out,
you are lost, at sea,
and then, if you're me,
your skin gets hot and itchy,
your face goes all twitchy
and you feel such a fool
and really hate school.
Singled out
you're about
to be laughed at
and you hate that.
Everyone else seems to know
and you want to go
straight home
to be alone.

Well, please don't despair –
life's not fair
but we all feel much the same.

So next time your hand shoots high
and you wonder why
your mind's gone blank,
just be honest, be frank.
Don't worry, don't even care.
Believe me, we've all been there.

WE'LL BE HERE AS LONG AS IT TAKES

Right, let's have the truth.
Which one of you did it?
Come on.
We haven't got all day.
The quicker someone owns up,
the easier it is for everyone else
and we can get on.

Well . . .
we'll be here as long as it takes.

Put your hand down, Morgan.
No, you're not going to the toilet.
Sit up straight, Siân.
It's not a slouching contest.
Colin, ceiling . . . eyes on me please.

I'm waiting.

As long as you waste my time
I shall waste yours.
It certainly doesn't look like
you'll be out for break.
You can sigh all you like, Dewi Miles.
I'm still waiting.

Let's see a hand please.
Stop smirking, Glenys Giles, it's not attractive.
One of you sitting there knows who did it,
maybe more than one of you.
Do not protect anyone.
They wouldn't protect you.
They have no moral courage
and I want the truth.
And the truth
always comes out in the end.

I'm waiting.
I'll ask one last time:

Who wrote 'I'm anonymous' on the board?

LIFE ON EARTH

It's the crunching, sun-drenched snow,
the warm lilac breeze,
a keen-eyed kestrel hovering overhead.
It's the rain-filled purple sky,
the tangled tree-top woods,
the fathomless, bottomless oceans,
the merging, melting ice caps,
the shrinking violets, the advancing deserts.
It's pond life, plant life, human life,
it's carnivores and conifers,
fossils and frogs.
It's microscopic, it's mammoth,
it's deforestation, it's preservation,
it's weeds and warts,
aubergines and aardvarks,
sharks and savannah,
coral and crime,
comedy and coal.
It's nature and nurture,
it's on us, it's in us,
it's survival, it's extinction.
It's them and us, you or me.
Grab it, caress it,
love it, enjoy it:
it's yours.

BISCUIT BREAK

Go on, risk it,
dunk a biscuit,
but be careful what you choose,
some you win, some you lose.
Custard Creams crumble,
Garibaldis grumble,
Rich Tea are so humble
they stumble and slide in
but don't even begin with shortbread –
they are just plain hard.
They laugh at hot tea
and after two hours you'll see
they're as rock solid as before.
In fact the more you dunk
and the more they're sunk
they keep on coming up the same.
So don't play their game
to try and dunk them tame –
just bite them in half instead!

END OF TERM

I wanted to get Miss a present
for the end of term
to thank her
and show how she's appreciated.
I wanted to get Miss a present,
but what to get?
Chocolates? Everyone gives those.
Wine? I can't get served.
A mug? She has a kitchen full of those.
A book? Science fiction, horror or romance?
I wanted to get Miss a present,
but what to get?
So I settled for an apple,
the oldest present of all.
It takes energy from fifty leaves to make one apple.
'An apple a day keeps the doctor away.'
And they float because 25% of their volume is air.
They fall because of gravity . . . ask Isaac Newton.
There are 7,500 varieties worldwide.
Snow White nearly died eating an apple
and, apparently, Eve spoilt it for everyone
by picking one.
So I'm giving Miss a Granny Smith
for her new
Core Curriculum.

A WARNING FROM THE AUTHOR

Please be warned that the title poem 'A Wee Bit of Trouble' is a completely true story. So that means Mrs Grimwood is (or was – some years have passed since I was in that assembly hall!) a real person.

She reminds me that teachers dictate the 'weather' in the classroom. They can make a child's life sunny or stormy. They can make learning fun or full of fear and failure. I like teachers who make it fun.

One way and another I've had quite a lot to do with schools – first as a pupil, then as a teacher and, nowadays, as a visiting poet. Along the way, I've played football, had children of my own and travelled in Africa and Asia . . . but reading and writing poetry has always been really important. And lots of poems have come out of my own experience.

I go to a lot of schools and other venues, such as play schemes, parks and prisons, and I'm always inspired by people who keep diaries, who love reading and who write their own poems and stories.

I've worked with many young people who want to listen and write on Saturday mornings or during their summer holidays. But there are many others who think they can't write poetry and I want to say to them: yes, you can!

Poems can be about anything and ideas can strike at any time – not just when other people ask you to write. Sometimes that's the very last thing you feel like doing but you might get the urge at some other time – usually when you haven't got pen or paper handy!

It seems to me school is just a part of it for all of us. We don't have to start and stop there. We play football or dance or juggle knives in our free time, so why can't we read and write then too? Just remember to keep diaries and notebooks handy.

So, keep reading and keep writing. You are now in a very special club that involves you and me and all the others who smile about life in – and out of – school.

I'm often called a performance poet. I think that means that I get invited to all kinds of places to stand up and perform my poems. I depend on my audience to laugh – and groan – in all the right places. If they don't, I know that either I need to do a bit of re-writing – or I need to improve my performance. I've put some tips on performing poetry in the next section.

I hope you enjoy reading these poems because I had a lot of fun writing them. I think poems are written to be read aloud so try them out, try them on. Read them in different ways, pause and hold a moment, try them softly, try them outside, try out the character of Mrs Grimwood – if you dare!

PERFORMING POETRY

A poet once said:

> 'Alas for those that never sing,
> but die with all their music inside them.'

We all need to sing our songs (or poems) and, at least once in our lives, shout some words from rooftops. Don't go through life without singing your own song and letting people know you're there. (Remember Timid Tina and Timid Tom ended up without any dinner . . . every day!)

So have a go at performing. It doesn't have to be in front of thousands but it could be in your living room to your gran, or in front of your class.

- Be prepared.

- Ask questions of the poem: what's it about? Are there funny bits? Sad bits? Your audience needs to get those feelings from you as you read it.

- Pause at planned moments. (Typing the poem on the computer helps. Double space it, print it out and mark up pauses and any other points you want to emphasise, with coloured highlighters.)

- Practise.

- Vary the tone of your voice (don't just be loud or quiet!). Try different voices for different parts.

- When you think you're ready, read through your material a couple of times if you don't already know it by heart. Actors spend hours preparing and so with poems too, it is great to learn them off by heart if you can.

- Look at your audience and smile. Introduce your performance and tell them what you'll be doing.

- Put everything into your performance.

And, above all, ENJOY IT!
(Remember everybody gets nervous.)

I know performing isn't everyone's cup of tea but in life we all have to do a bit of it, so it is worth working at. And it's not rocket science either!

Be confident! I believe in you and I know those around you do too, so go on, go out there and write your words, sing your song, perform your poem, give it your all . . . and it doesn't matter who's watching . . . even if it's Mrs Grimwood!